the Lost Sock

Gillian Johnson

For
Nick and Nova

the Lost Sock

Gillian Johnson

CONSTABLE

CONSTABLE

First published in Great Britain in 2014 by Constable

Copyright Gillian Johnson, 2014

A CIP catalogue record for this book
is available from the British Library.

UK ISBN: 978-1-47211-243-9 (hardback)
UK ISBN: 978-1-47211-250-7 (ebook)

Typesetting and design in London by Design 23
Printed and bound in China by C&C Joint Printing Co

Constable
is an imprint of
Constable & Robinson Ltd
100 Victoria Embankment
London EC4Y 0DY

An Hachette UK Company
www.hachette.co.uk

www.constablerobinson.com

'I could really use a new
pair of socks!'

'It's good to get socks with a pattern,
because they won't get lost in the wash!'

'Awesome
socks.'

'Oops!'

'Maybe someone can
help me.'

'You can share my washer and dryer!'

'Well, bye now.'

'Oh no!'

'Just one sock!'

'I loved that sock.'

'Maybe she's taken it!'

'Could I wear odd socks?'

'Too dark.'

'Too spotty.'

'Too boring.'

'No. There is only one perfect match.'

'Sorry, you bought the last pair.'

'No sign of it here.'

'I really loved
that sock.'

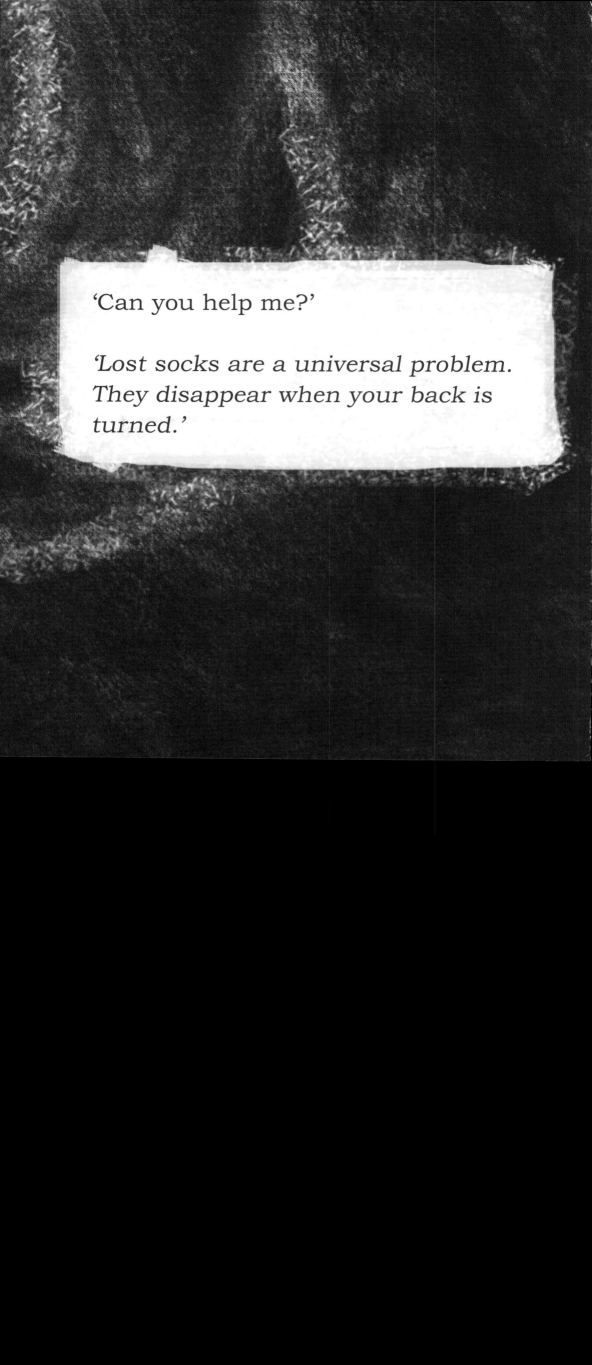

'Can you help me?'

*'Lost socks are a universal problem.
They disappear when your back is
turned.'*

'And for some reason, you'll always lose the sock you love most.'

'But why? Where do they all go'

'Some experts think that the socks are
sucked through a portal in the back
of the tumble dryer, where they
enter a wormhole . . .'

'. . . arriving, eventually, on
The Planet of Lost Socks.'

'Some think they make their
way to a forest on the
Turkish-Bulgarian border . . .'

'. . . while others claim that they end up in children's playgroups, where they make excellent puppets.'

'Puppets?
Where did I see that poster?'

'I must go!'

'*That* is my sock!
'You found it in the
laundry basket'

'But I need it for
the show!'

'Although I suppose . . .'

'. . . they do
belong together.'

'It would be sad for them to
be parted ever again.'

'Yes, it really would.'

'They really are awesome socks.'